The World Conference in Heaven

Kyuka Lilymjok

ISBN: *ISBN* 978-978-954-757-9

Published by:
Free Pen Publishers
10 Lachlan Close Maitama, Abuja

Any people depicted in stock imagery provided by Think stock are models, and such images are being used for such purposes only.

This book is printed on acid-free paper.

The views expressed in this work are solely those of the author and do not necessarily reflect the views of the publisher. The publisher hereby disclaims any responsibility for them.

To the god of freethinkers

It is not sick
But healthy to laugh
At the human condition

Passage One

For some days, a mournful atmosphere hung over heaven. God was not speaking to anyone. Angels who usually sang, danced and clapped, stopped singing, dancing and clapping because God was not responding to any of their yaps and theatrics. Something was wrong. God was thinking, and any time God thought, something bad happened. The first time he thought before now, a storm, no one knew its origin burst on heaven. Many angels were tossed out of heaven and were never seen again. The second and last time he thought, heaven shook with thunder and brimstone. After the thunder and brimstone many angels were also missing.

After the second thinking of God that brought thunder and brimstone, angels started wondering whether, now and then, God cleansed heaven of miscreants using, not his heavy hand, but his mighty mind that caused upheavals of cataclysmic proportion. But how could God be cleansing heaven leaving the earth, which had become an Augean stable of sort? Or had he finally given up on the earth, abandoning it to the devil?

Now God was thinking again. Was he about cleansing heaven for a third time, or was he finally coming round to cleansing the earth? Angels wondered. Rather than clean the earth however, God called a world conference in heaven. Angels were shocked and visibly angry. What pranks was God playing, calling a world conference in heaven when he knew the presence of men, in their sinful state, would defile heaven? Could it be the angels that were tossed out of heaven by the storm, or that went missing after the thunder and brimstone were staging a comeback through the conference?

Passage Two

The news of the world conference in heaven was received with excitement in various cities, towns and villages around the world. In the forest and the air, birds were jubilant for they too had been invited to the conference and would send a delegation. Man was about perishing the earth with his greed and gluttony. Very thoughtful of God, the birds chirped and ululated. Of course, were they to confer with angels on the thoughtfulness of God, they might have found the latter not so excited.

As ecstatic as people were about the conference, there were few people that were not so excited. Such people saw little need for the conference. Shortly after news of the conference was received on earth, one of the non-enthusiasts met with an enthusiast, and the two began talking about the conference.

'Honestly, I can't understand what all the noise about the conference in heaven is all about,' said the non-enthusiast.

'Honestly, I also cannot understand your lack of enthusiasm in the conference,' said the enthusiast. 'Given what is happening in the world today, where but at a conference in heaven can it be tackled?'

'At least so you think.'

'How do you think?'

'I think the world will remain the world, conference or no conference.'

'I think the world would be heaven, if now and then, we have conferences in heaven to sort out things on earth.'

'Who told you things are sorted out in heaven itself?' said the non-enthusiast. 'Things, anywhere you go, are nasty and I don't think talking about them will change anything.'

'I think differently,' said the enthusiast. 'I think talking about things will make a difference. It will put sense in senseless people who are destroying the earth.'

Passage Three

To lead the world delegation to the world conference in heaven, God appointed Banju, a black man. There was palpable resentment among white people of God's choice of a black man as leader of the delegation.

'There is no black prophet, why should a black man lead the delegation to heaven?' Forsyth, chosen by whites to lead their delegation fumed.

'Precisely what entitles him to leadership of the delegation,' God said. 'If I have not been fair before, I want to be now. If all the prophets are white, it is fair that on this minor and transient matter of a conference in heaven, a black man leads the delegation. Fairness apart, there is also gratitude in my action. Though not having prophets, blacks have displayed more faith in me. They have kept my name on earth. But for this conference, white people have almost all forgotten about me.'

'How are the mighty fallen?' Forsyth mourned. 'Will the rejected stone end up the cornerstone?'

'Don't see it that way my child,' God consoled

'The black man can only lead a delegation to hell,' Forsyth murmured.

Well, God did not hear him.

Ordinarily, a clergy man would have been appointed to lead the delegation to heaven; but the world had become too wary of clergies. They couldn't be relied on to ask God some basic questions.

Birds were also not happy with God's choice of the delegation's leader. The leader should have been a bird. They too have no prophet, Silhawk, the leader of the birds' delegation protested. What is more, if God had appointed a bird, he wouldn't have acrimony among birds on choice of color.

Before God could say anything, Banju pointed out to the birds that angels are birds, and so birds were not as badly off as black men.

'I wasn't speaking to you; so, hold your peace,' Silhawk Shrieked in anger.

'You are in the sky with me,' God consoled the birds. 'You don't really need this leadership.'

'Men are also in the sky with you in their aircraft,' Silhawk said, still not pacified. 'It is even in their aircraft they would attend the conference.'

'Yes, men may occasionally be in the air with me; but how much of me can they know being in an aircraft?' God said. 'Not so birds. You are always in the sky with me and hear my voice all the time.'

'In all these we are not talking about the animals,' said Banju. 'They also are entitled to attend the conference.'

'They have not been invited,' said Silhawk.

'If they were invited, how will they attend?'

'That would have been up to their devices.'

'Maybe they will hitch a ride in men's aircraft,' a bird said.

'Ssh ...,' Silhawk, belatedly, tried to hush the bird that just spoke. 'Are you out of your mind?' he asked the bird, heatedly. 'Don't you know if men carry animals to the conference in their aircraft, animals so carried will be hostages at the conference toeing the line of men on every issue or else they would be abandoned in heaven by their benefactors?' he asked the bird in a voice that carried a whip.

'Wolves, hyenas and bush pigs abandoned in heaven? That would be very bad for God and his angels,' the bird that made the suggestion said, shrinking its body in revulsion. 'Sorry I did not think of all the implications,' it said in a meek tone.

'If birds must stop men using a bird's brain as a synonym of stupidity, birds must think before talking,' Silhawk said without let in his anger.

'Well, if animals can't make it to the conference in heaven, maybe God will come down to the earth and hold another conference with them after the heaven conference,' Banju said, breaking the discussion between the two birds.

Passage Four

Delegates started arriving heaven two days to the conference. Neither God nor his angels had expected this, and so had not made arrangements to receive the delegates. God had expected delegates to arrive on the day the conference would start to save cost on accommodation and feeding, only to see delegates trooping in two days to the conference. Despite the fact that he was not prepared for their arrival, God, being the lord of host, was able to provide accommodation and feeding for the unexpected guests. Only that his angels deployed to arrange accommodations had to run around like chickens with their heads cut off.

Delegates to the conference from the earth were surprised to see in heaven dead people they expected to be in hell. Some of these people were not only in heaven, they were there as archangels.

'So, you made heaven,' a conferee asked an archangel he knew was a bad man while on earth.

'You thought I will make hell?' the archangel asked, irritably.

'If there is a place worse than hell, you should have made it,' the conferee said. 'After cleaning out our treasury as Prime Minister, assassinating and killing hundreds of our people, you should not only be in hell, you should rot there.'

'Before I died, I repented of my sins.'

'Of what use is your repentance to those you cheated?'

'Well, here I am in heaven, not even as a commoner, but as a Prime Minister of sort. You seem to forget that as it is on earth, it is in heaven. I not only made heaven, I made it as the Prime Minister I was on earth.'

'Something must be going on behind God's back here,' the delegate said more to himself than to the archangel.

The archangel moved on, leaving the confounded delegate. Still in his astonishment, another dead person he knew walked past him.

'Hi,' the man said.

'H...i,' the delegate said, raising his hand lamely. 'Are you also in heaven?' he asked. This was the man that killed his son.

'Well, let's say I sneaked into this conference. I didn't quite make heaven.'

I thought as much. God cannot be so unfair? Even that evil man that claimed he made heaven because he repented must have sneaked into heaven. But, how can God allow inmates of hell to sneak into heaven? he wondered in despair. The conference will not achieve much if agents of the devil are sneaking into it or even eavesdropping on it. The devil is not new on torpedoing God's plans.

'Why are you looking so depressed?' another delegate asked the one that was shocked by people he was seeing in heaven.

'I am seeing what I thought I will not see in heaven,' the first delegate said.

'What are you seeing?'

'I am finding in heaven people I knew on earth to be the devil's assistants,' said the first conferee.

'I thought I was the only one in this nightmare,' said the second man. 'It is so dismaying. What then is the incentive of being good?'

'To make matters worse, I am yet to see Showel; surely he couldn't have missed heaven with so much faith.'

'He could if evil men are making it. This is a place of surprises and shock.'

As the two men stood talking, they were approached by a man from the same town with the second delegate. This man, while on earth, was rumored to be a Satanist. He had no wife and no children. He lived with his parents well into his forties. His father was suffering from the Parkinson disease while his mother was suffering from acute arthritis. One day he hacked both parents to death then impaled himself on a sword. It was the most gruesome thing his town had ever witnessed. Now he was in heaven.

'Bonshe, how did it happen?' the second delegate asked the man.

'How did what happen?' the man asked in turn.

'How did you make heaven?'

'I showed mercy to my parents by killing them, and showed mercilessness to myself by killing myself. Mercy to others, mercilessness to yourself are the two things you need to make heaven.'

'Honestly, I don't understand you.'

'What is important is that God understood me.'

'This is incredible.'

'Yet, here it is. You see, God does not like seeing suffering. At the same time, he cannot kill those that are suffering to end their suffering. Whoever takes suffering from the sight of God, however he does so, earns God's gratitude. This was what earned me heaven. Again, God likes a man with the heart of a lion. What I did showed guts. With all his defects of character, David earned God's favor because of his courage. With God, courage trumps all things.'

'Murder and suicide are crimes.'

'Before man, yes. Before God murder is a sin only when the person killed is enjoying life. If he is suffering life, God rewards his killer with heaven. Suicide is no crime to God. Whoever kills himself shows he no longer enjoys life and God is happy with him for taking misery from his sight.'

Passage Five

Delegates from the earth were surprised to find that God called the conference for a reason different from reasons they supposed. While they supposed God called the conference because he was not happy with conditions on earth, he called the conference because he had heard there was an imminent invasion of the earth and heaven by alien enemies.

Based on the reasons they thought the conference was called, delegates from the earth went to the conference with agendas God never contemplated. Depending on their perceived afflictions or problems, nations and races of the world went to the conference to ask God why their conditions were what they were.

Because delegates were not prepared for God's agenda for the conference; because God was not prepared for their queries, the conference had an uneasy start, but eventually settled into lively and comic deliberations.

Passage Six

On the day of the conference, God appeared before conferees in a sheet of cloud. Conferees that had thought they would see God in person were disappointed by this. For a while, there were stirs and drones among conferees.

'What is the meaning of the funny expressions I see on their faces and the mumblings coming from their lips,' an angel whispered to another angel. 'I hope they have not brought their witchcraft here.'

'They dare not,' the other angel whispered back. 'If they do, they would not be tossed out of heaven to earth; they would be tossed out to hell direct.'

'Yes, they will be tossed out to hell to be hugged by the devil the way he hugs a witch,' said the first angel.

Amidst the mild commotion caused by God appearing in a sheet of cloud, God placed his agenda for the confab before conferees. For a while no one spoke. Shock was visible on the faces of conferees. This was not the agenda they were expecting. When they overcame their shock,

Forsyth asked how God came by his apprehension that aliens will invade heaven and the earth.

'The wind told me.'

'You mean the idle wind?'

'It may be the idle wind to you, it is the busy wind to me. If you don't know, it was the wind I used to create the world.'

'The wind?'

'Yes, the wind.'

'You mean the rascal and wayward wind?'

'It may be the rascal and wayward wind to you; for me it is the purposeful wind.'

'No wonder the earth is so rascal and wayward.'

God did not say anything.

And what did you use to create the wind?'

Again, God did not say anything. He did not even appear to have heard what was said.

'I even wonder who created you and what he used to create you,' Forsyth said in a waggish voice.

'Infidel!' a conferee screamed. 'You will pay with your life for this blasphemy. Imagine the crude impudence of the infidel!'

'Ssh ...' God hushed the enraged conferee.

'Allow me to kill the vermin!'

'Not here,' God said.

'Not here? So, he can kill me elsewhere?' Forsyth asked with a faltering heart.

'Well, I haven't exactly said so.'

'Oh my God!'

'So, you have God.'

You see why I could not make you delegation leader, God thought, his mind on Forsyth. Even without making you leader, how am I going to fare in this conference with a mind like yours? Perhaps I shouldn't have invited you at all. But what sort of conference would it have been without you? Switching his mind from Forsyth, he began speaking to the conferees again: 'When I wanted to create the seas, I sent the wind to gather all the water droplets in the air and deposit them on earth as the seas. When I wanted to create the earth, I sent the wind to gather all the dust particles in the air and deposit them as the earth. After creating the seas and the earth, I asked the wind to produce beast, bird and man from moist dust particles in the air.'

'Wonderful; so you did not say, "let there be water, and there was water, or let there be light and there was light" as we have been made to think,' Forsyth said in apparent amazement.

'If I speak into existence, it was the wind that I used to do so. Whatever word I used to create things was thrown on the wind and the wind carried it into effect,' God said in a buoyant voice.

'So the word was the wind and the wind was the word,' Forsyth said, scathingly.

'More or less like that,' God said, tersely.

'Ah this life!' Forsyth exclaimed, looking a little befuddled. 'It is so difficult knowing who or what to trust. The dividing line between what we see as rascal and what we see as responsible is so thin that one sometimes needs a microscope to see it.'

'Do you know where the aliens will be coming from?' a conferee asked, steering discussion back to the agenda of the conference.

'If God does not know, who will know?' said Banju.

'If God does not know the devil will know,' murmured Silhawk. 'After all the aliens must be coming at his behest.'

'What of the wind; does it know where the aliens will be coming from?' asked Forsyth.

'The wind is not sure. It said they might be coming from Thongos — a universe light years away from heaven and earth. As we are talking, the aliens might already be on their way to us. But because of the distance between Thongos and where we are, it will take them two years from now to get here.'

Passage Seven

The Conference hall was seized by fear. For a moment, a buzz of murmurs and whispers filled the hall as conferees expressed their anxieties and fears.

'The invasion is that imminent?' a conferee asked of no one.

'It is,' God replied.

'What do we do?' Banju asked.

'That's why I called the conference,' God said. 'I called the conference so that we can put our heads together to evolve a strategy of repelling the aliens.'

'If the aliens succeed at invading the earth and heaven, what will become of the earth and heaven?' Forsyth asked.

'There will be a new earth, a new heaven and a new God,' God said.

'In that case we have nothing to worry about,' said Forsyth. 'I am tired of the present earth.'

"And the present God,' said a conferee at the back of the conference hall. A new earth and a new God will just be fine with me.'

'Infi...,' a conferee began to say but stopped himself. God is listening to the infidel, he thought. If he would allow such profanity, so be it.

'I am with you,' someone said in support of the conferee who said a new earth and a new God would be fine with him. 'This is not our fight. This is God's fight. Let him fight his fight. This is God's headache; let him find medicine for it. I have my own headaches and I am taking care of them the best way I can. If this is what the conference is all about, I wish to be excused.'

'You fools! You will be wiped away with the old earth; that is what God is saying,' another conferee said.

'What!'

'Yes. The old earth will not go alone. You will escort it into extinction.'

'*Uhime calamite*!'

'Blockheads!'

'Let's break up for a while and assemble later,' God said drifting away in the sheet of cloud he spoke to the conferees.

Passage Eight

It was not long before the conference was in session again. God looked much cheerful than he was before the short break. So did many conferees. The initial disquiet of the conference caused mainly by dashed expectations of conferees from the earth had receded and the conference was settling down to business.

'God, I propose the wind that brought news of the aliens' invasion be used against the aliens. If you used it to create the earth and heaven, you can use it to save them from destruction,' Forsyth said when the conference settled down to business.

The way this guy's mind works is dreadful, God thought. 'The wind cannot be used against the aliens because in a way they are wind. Indeed, the wind said they will invade heaven and earth in a tumultuous wind.'

So, the wind is reporting on the wind? Forsyth thought. Really strange. To God he said, 'if the wind they come in is a cold wind and I think that will likely be the case, we will set a wind of fire upon them.'

'You are saying something there,' said a conferee. 'We will send the fire of hell to combat them. The devil needs to be invited to this conference since he is in charge of hell. Soon we may need to tap from his resources.'

'You are right,' said another conferee. 'Apart from being in charge of hell, when it comes to dealing with sinister designs, no one compares with the devil. The devil is as devilish as anyone you know.'

'What are you guys saying?' an angel screamed in disbelief. 'Do you know where you are?'

'We are in heaven before God who created the devil and hell,' the conferee who first said the devil should be invited replied, unruffled.

I suspected this from the very beginning of this conference thought the angel that just spoke. There is no way these guys will come here without their witchcraft. Invite the devil to the conference so that he can hug you the way he hugs a witch, enh? Well, I won't say anything more. God asked for it; he is getting it.

'Invite the devil?' another angel exclaimed in shock. 'Do you know who that guy is? Well, I guess you won't know because he is not your neighbor.'

'Well, gentlemen, let's calm down,' God said. 'No one is inviting the devil to the conference. The devil is my neighbor. If I thought he could help, I wouldn't have summoned you all the way from the earth.'

'So, it was a summon,' murmured a conferee to a neighbor. 'I thought it was an invitation.'

'What does it matter whether it was a summon or an invitation?' the neighbor said. 'The important thing is that you are here to help solve a problem; help solve it. By the way, God is God; he cannot only summon you, he can arrest you. So, what are you saying?'

'Let's have some order,' cooed the angel God appointed to serve as the conference clerk.

A hush fell on the conference.

Passage Nine

'The devil will not be invited to this conference,' God affirmed again.

'We heard you the first time,' a conferee whispered to another conferee.

'The devil might not be invited, but we have been seeing his inmates sneaking into the conference,' a fat conferee whispered to a wispy looking conferee. 'If his agents are sneaking in uninvited, what stops him? For all God may not know the devil is already in this conference sitting right behind him

'That cannot be,' whispered the wispy conferee. 'God must have an ADC. He would not allow the devil to sit behind God.'

'I have not seen any ADC behind God,' whispered the fat conferee.

'Neither have you seen God. All you are seeing is a sheet of cloud. The ADC might be the air behind God,' retorted the wispy conferee.

Let's have some order in this conference!' spat the conference clerk.

There was silence once more.

'Without the devil, the conference will find means to deal with the impending threat,' God continued speaking.

'How? remains the question,' Forsyth quipped.

'Yes, how? Perhaps you came with the how from the earth,' God said.

'Even when it is here we learned of the disease, we could have come with the cure from the earth?' Forsyth said with a mild sardonic expression.

'You are Forsyth,' an angel interposed.

'A seer you should have said,' Forsyth retorted.

'Alright gentlemen, calm down,' a man in Forsyth's delegation said, peremptorily. 'We are not without wits. We will come up with something.'

'We are waiting,' said an angel.

'We will heat the seas to water vapors. The invading aliens from Thongos would be singed by the welling water vapors of the seas,' said a conferee.

'That will not do,' said an angel. 'What of your stockpile of nuclear, biological and chemical weapons?' an angel asked. 'This might be when they will find use.'

'Those weapons are useless to the extent that the person using them is as much in danger of annihilation as the enemy,' said a conferee.

'Those weapons promise only a new heaven and a new earth,' another conferee said, jocularly.

'If the weapons cannot be used, why then did you make them?' an angel asked.

'Because we are stupid,' said another conferee.

'Holy Mackerel!'

'No, holy smoke!'

'We are in for it.'

'No, we are out for it.'

Passage Ten

'Gentlemen, back to the matter in conference,' a conferee tried to steer the conference back to the question of the proper defense to the impending invasion.

'We will invite aliens from Fagasso a universe superior to Thongos to engage the invading aliens from Thongos,' said an angel. 'It will be a war of aliens and I have no doubt that Fagasso will triumph over Thongos.'

'There is a lot in what you said,' God said; 'and it is worthy of this conference's deliberations.'

'Because it is from an angel, there would be a lot in it,' a short conferee snickered to a tall conferee. 'I have a feeling we were invited to this conference to be rubbished.'

'No need for such bitterness and suspicion,' said the tall conferee. 'We should look at the merit of what is said, not who said it.'

The conference deliberated on the suggestion of the angel to use aliens from Fagasso to ward off the invading aliens of Thongos. In the end, it was agreed by the conference that the proposed defense could be used to repel the invasion.

Passage Eleven

The conference delegation from the earth then pleaded with God to be allowed to make submissions to him on their problems on earth though their submissions were not the reason God called the conference. God obliged them saying their submissions could be taken under *Any Other Business*.

'*Any other business*,' mused a conferee. 'Those on earth who thought we are the business, should hear God: we are merely *any other business*.'

Banju as leader of the world delegation placed the worries, concerns and fears of the world before the conference. Top on the list were religious bigotry, terrorism and racial discrimination. Outside these common concerns of the world, there were particular concerns of the various races of the world and the birds.

The conference deliberated on religious bigotry first. While religion seemed to be cooling off in certain quarters, it was burning like phosphorus in others. Why was this the case? God was asked.

'Well, people do not understand me the same way,' God said.

'Probably because you have not revealed yourself to them the same way,' remarked a conferee.

'Often, people hear what they want to hear, not what I said,' God enthused.

'Well, well, this is something,' Forsyth murmured.

'This means some of what is written in the holy writs is not exactly what you said,' a conferee said.

'You bet,' God replied, rapidly.

'So, prophets like pastors and imams are not to be trusted,' the conferee that spoke last said. 'This is surely something.'

'The devil you are great,' whispered a conferee to his neighbor.

'Mind what you say and where you say it,' the neighbor said.

'If prophets cannot be trusted, who can one trust?' a conferee wondered rhetorically.

'You can trust God.'

'Are you sure of that?'

'Well, I can't be too sure. But you must trust someone.'

'Based on their prejudices and preferences, prophets heard from me what they wanted to hear not what I said,' God began talking again.

A hush fell on the conference hall.

'As prophets heard from me what they wanted to hear,' God continued talking, 'people professing to follow me understand me the way they want to understand me. Because people do not understand me the same way, their attitudes towards me differ. There are those who think I am a consuming flame of fire and so in their seeking to advance my case among men, they behave like erupting volcanoes. They are wrong. I am not a fire-spiting monster. If I were, you would have begun to see my fire in this conference. Then there are those who think I don't exist because I am too quiet for them to hear and too invisible for them to see. This set of people does not even bother to believe in me. They are also wrong. I exist.'

'We are not sure about that,' a conferee said. 'If indeed you exist, some of us will like to see you in this conference and not merely hear your voice in a sheet of cloud.'

'Imagine going back to earth and people asking you what God looks like and you saying though you were with him throughout a conference, you don't know what he looks like,' said a conferee.

'You can say he looks like a sheet of cloud,' another conferee retorted, cynically.

'Holy smoke!'

'You can say he looks like the devil,' whispered a conferee to a neighbor. But the neighbor did not say anything. He did not even appear to have heard what he said.

'What! Has the devil taken over my senses?' the whispering conferee whispered again, in apparent shock and awe of what he whispered.

'You are on your own,' his neighbor said, finally. 'I didn't hear a word of what you said.'

'It is for your own good that I speak to you in a cloud. You cannot behold my face and live,' God said.

'We are tired of hearing that,' someone hissed.

'I am slow to anger.'

'We are also tired of hearing that.'

There was a blast of thunder. The conference room shook. Men and birds shrunk in fear.

Passage Twelve

'Well, well God, you exist. I have never had any doubts about that,' said Forsyth. 'If I had, I wouldn't have turned up for this conference. But I don't think you should prove your existence the way you just did, particularly before the religious fanatics amongst us. If before witnessing your might the way they just did, they had not forgotten to be fire-spitting monsters, what will they be after witnessing it?'

'They will remember I was pushed to anger,' God said.

'And forget not to blast us out of existence if they think we are contravening you?' mourned a conferee yet to overcome his fear.

'God, you need to give the fanatics among us a message to take back home. I don't think the one you just gave is the right one,' a conferee whined.

'And you think the infidels don't need a message to take home?' said a conferee in a voice reeking violence.

'They have already received one. The thunder was a message, or do you want God to dip them in hell so that they take the scars to the world as a message?' asked a conferee.

'That won't be a bad idea,' said a conferee with a ferocious voice and a face that bore an expression of bad temper. 'For their reformation, infidels should be singed now and then.'

'See what I am saying,' a conferee said, turning to God. 'Only two words come out of the mouth of a fanatic: *infidel, kill*. He is calling us *infidels* now. The next thing he will say is *kill*. 'God, please say something.'

'I am God. I can fight my own fight,' God said.

'You just proved that,' a conferee said.

'Those who kill others in defense of me may think they are honoring me, but in truth are dishonoring and pouring contempt on me. They are saying I am too weak to fight for myself or even that I don't exist.'

'I hope they have a modicum of intelligence to understand you,' said Forsyth.

'While they may think they are showing contempt for those they kill in my defense, they are in fact showing respect and reverence to them. They are saying that such persons are stronger than me and so have to kill them on my behalf.'

'Where are the terrorists raping and killing in God's name?' Forsyth said. 'God is saying you are losing with men and losing with him. Perhaps the only person you are winning with is the devil.'

'Whoever believes in me, should believe in my power. Indeed, without my power why should anyone believe in me? Without the poison of the snake why should anyone fear it? If belief in me is founded on my power, then believers in me should allow my power to fight for me. If they choose to fight for me, they don't believe in my powers and to the extent of this unbelief are in truth infidels.'

'God, you are God!' a conferee ululated.

'Are you just knowing that?' someone said.

'I have always known it, but slept on it. What he just said has woken me up to what I have always known.'

Passage Thirteen

On the third day of the conference, deliberations shifted to racism which is a form of terrorism. It is a form of terrorism because it has the same effect with terrorism: it cows its victim.

Whites have treated us quite unfairly,' a black conferee said. 'They have treated us as if we are toilet paper.'

'If we think, you are toilet paper, we will make the toilet paper black, not white,' said a white conferee.

'Whites have treated us as if we are Ebola,' said another black conferee.

'Are you not?' charged a white delegate.

'God, you see what we are saying? Even before you, they can't hide their contempt for us which, in a way, is contempt for you because you created us.'

'Don't incite God against us,' a white conferee protested.

'No one can incite God against you without your contribution.'

'God knows we revere him.'

'Then show it.'

'If, in your mind, we can only show our reverence for God by respecting the black man, you missed the point. If we must tell you the truth, we don't believe God created the black man, at least not the God we are before.'

'Who created him?'

'You may ask the devil.'

'I will not ask the devil; I am asking you.'

'I have not been told I am the devil's spokesman.'

'But you just spoke for him; in fact, you spoke like him.'

'God is light. Whoever is not light is not likely to be the *own* of God.'

'The devil is dark. Whoever is dark is likely to be the *own* of the devil.'

'I believe by darkness you only think of skin darkness. But there is a worse darkness — that of the heart, which I can see in you. God does not work with the skin, but the heart. Your heart being so dark, you are the *own* of the devil not minding the whiteness of your skin.'

'As the devil is dark, I believe hell is also dark. If this conference were holding in hell, it will hold in darkness and we will all go back without seeing the face of the devil,' said a white conferee.

'He is speaking as if he has seen the face of God,' someone said.

'I have not seen his face, but he has good reason not showing his face.'

'Who told you the devil has no better reason.'

'Holy Moses!'

'I am still wondering how some people were invited to this conference. They should be invited only to a conference called by the devil,' said a white conferee.

'Who said we should invite the devil to the conference? Was it not a black man?' asked another white conferee.

'God, please say something,' pleaded a black conferee.

'What do you want him to say? To tell two barking dogs to stop barking?' asked an angel.

'No, to assert paternity.'

'The black man looks like a charred escapee from hell.'

'And what do you look like; a whitewash?'

'What gives respect is behavior. If blacks put up better behavior than we know with them, we will respect them. Respect, we all know is like money; it is earned.'

'I am father of all,' God spoke at last.

'Does all include the devil?' someone asked.

God ignored him and continued; 'because I am father of all, I invited all to this conference.'

'Where are the animals?' someone asked.

Again, God ignored him, and continued talking. 'You only give birth to a child; you don't give birth to his behavior. The behavior of a child is given birth to by how he understands life. If he has a good understanding of life, he will behave well. If he has a bad understanding of life, he will behave badly.'

'Who gives birth to understanding?' someone asked.

God ignored him.

'Why is God always ignoring things?' someone complained, bitterly. 'The same attitude we lament about him on earth, he is putting up before us in heaven.'

'It is this same attitude of God not speaking out when he should that has led some people into saying he does not exist,' somebody lamented.

'To make his existence felt, God should intervene when he should,' another person supported the last person who spoke.

'Silence is golden.'

'When speaking is necessary, silence is less than bronze.'

'I believe behavior is a gene thing,' a conferee tried to steer discussion back to why blacks and whites behave the way they do.

'And who do you think gives birth to genes?'

'The person who creates the human being of course!' someone exclaimed. 'He creates the genes the same way he creates the feet. Both the genes and the feet are his craft. If they are twisted, he is to blame. If they are well formed, he is to praise.'

Passage Fourteen

There was a long lightning and a loud blast of thunder that sounded like a bomb explosion. God has been in a thoughtful silence for a while. Anytime he was silent and became thoughtful in the course of the conference, angels held their breath. They knew what his thinking could bring, if the visitors from the earth did not.

The intensity of the thunder threw some conferees off their seats. The conference hall was alive with terror, panic and commotion. No conferee had sufficient calm to speak or even to hear anything.

'God, you are God, we don't need further proof,' Forsyth moaned when he had regained some composure. 'When we get back to earth, we will tell the doubting Thomases there is God. 'Please, we don't need further proof in the way of what just happened,' he pleaded on his knees.

'God, we are sorry, please forgive us,' pleaded another conferee also on his knees. 'To err is human. To forgive is divine.'

Almost all the conferees were now on their knees pleading with God to have mercy, to forgive.

Among the few conferees still on their seats, some were wondering whether the terror generated by the thunder was not a bad message to terrorists like the earlier thunder was thought to be a bad message to religious fanatics.

'I have heard you, erring children,' God spoke at last. 'I had no intention for this show of power, but for your behavior which I know you did not get from me, but from your misunderstanding of what life requires of you.'

Conferees that had recovered from the effect of the thunder wondered why God should be pushed to anger by mere mortals. Conferees yet to recover could only nod their heads to what God was saying.

Passage Fifteen

After racism, deliberations shifted to the Arabs and Israelis on the fourth day of the conference. Palestinian Arabs complained that Israelis were roasting them like yam though they were supposed to be brothers.

'The more reason, we should be at war,' an Israeli conferee said. 'Beginning with Cain and Abel the first brothers, the major wars from the beginning of time to now has been between brothers.'

'The Wantong people have a saying that why should I hate you when you are not my brother?' remarked a conferee.

'Between brothers, there is contempt bred by familiarity and envy bred by rivalry. These are potent causes of conflict,' said a conferee.

'The root cause of the Arab-Israeli conflict goes to Isaac and Ismael their progenitors,' someone said.

'I agree,' another person said. 'The two half-brothers were conceived and delivered in woeful circumstances that spelled war.'

'Can you recall anything the two did together, good or bad?' asked yet another person.

'Honestly, I cannot,' said a conferee with a comic visage. 'Raising the issue now, I can't remember any report of the two even knowing each other. Though half-brothers, they seemed strangers. That was the extent of the enmity between them.'

'The rivalry and bitterness of their mothers rubbed off on them,' said yet another person.

The conferees went on speaking without let or hindrance in a free for all talking session.

'The only way to resolve the Arab-Israeli conflict is to exhume the bones of Ishmael and Isaac and reconcile them.'

'You are forgetting the bones of their mothers. There was so much rivalry and bitterness between them.'

'Among the Nuer people of South Sudan, we will be in perpetual enmity if any of yours kills any of mine. The bones of the slain man will forever be between the two families until an earth priests dissolves them in an atonement ritual. There are bones between the Arabs and the Israelis. Until they are dissolved by an earth priest, all the peace talks are what they are – hot air and the idle wind.'

'You still call the wind idle even after been told it created the earth?'

'If the wind is idle after such work, who is busy?'

'Israelis are treating Arabs like maids.'

'Hagar was Sarah's maid.'

'Was she only a maid? She was her slave?'

'Let's not rake up the dirt of yesterday.'

'The dirt of yesterday is needed to tell some people who they are.'

'Palestinian Arabs deserve a break from the Israelis,' a conferee said in a loud voice trying to put deliberations back on track.

'Yes, Palestinians deserve a better deal from the Israelis,' someone supported the person that just spoke.

'You assume Israelis already have a better deal from Palestinians or that they will after giving Palestinians a better deal,' an Israeli said.

'He is speaking from ignorance,' said another Israeli. 'The Jew and the Arab believe in an eye for an eye. We will all be blind in Israel if we give Palestinians the better deal you are talking about. They will insist on plucking out all our eyes for their eyes we have plucked or think we have plucked. When it comes to vengeance, the Arab has no equal.'

'For two mad men to walk together, one must be humble,' someone said.

'And why should two mad men walk together. They are better off walking separately. I think even the world is better off with them walking separately,' replied an Israeli conferee.

'They are walking separately and the world is faring so badly; how will it fare if they walk together?' said another Israeli.

'The Arabs don't even spare themselves. If they can do what they are doing to themselves in Syria and Iraq, what will they not do to the Israelis?' said yet another Israeli conferee.

'Arabs are stabbing themselves out of frustration. Frustration can turn a man against himself,' said an Arab conferee.

Again, all conferees began talking without order or restrain.

'The only place on earth God says the devil has been to is the Middle East. It appears he never left. He has since made the Middle East his operational headquarters.'

'Is the Middle East Middle Hell?'

'Ssh ..., we are not far from hell. The devil may be listening in. You may not leave this place back to earth the way you are carrying on.'

'Why should I be in front of God and fear the devil?'

'Ask God first if he does not fear the devil.'

'Producing all the prophets, Jews and Arabs are supposed to be the immediate children of God, children of the covenant. As the special children of God who is peace, they are supposed to be more peaceful; why are they turning out children of war and fractious dissention?'

'With the peals of thunder we have gone through here, I wonder if God is peaceful.'

'Ssh ...'

Passage Sixteen

Conferees observed that God had not spoken since deliberations began on the Arab/Israeli conflict. He had been restless with thoughts. Angels were apprehensive. After a long while of silence, God chuckled then laughed. His laughter was both guttural and metallic. 'I am too sore to comment on the Jews and Arabs conflicts,' he said. 'Neither will I comment on their claims to be special people; but any of my angels may.'

'The Israeli/Arab conflict will continue until Israelis and Arabs stop making funny claims and start making gracious concessions; until they trade rigidity for compromise, pride for humility,' said an angel. 'Until they stop listening to the devil who keeps telling them who they are not, they will remain hosts to insurrections. The devil reaps war by sowing discord; fuels feuds by foisting feudalism. The discord, feuds and feudalism he sows and fuels among Jews and Arabs are divine claims to land and pride from claims of being God's special people because they produced prophets. God is the God of all nations, not the God of people who produced servants of God sent by God to serve his people. It is strange that people who produced servants are claiming to be masters. Since when did the maid become the princess?'

'What I am hearing is cool and soothing,' said a conferee with great delight. 'There you are saying you are God's special people, but have no land in a world God created full of lands. It is all very ridiculous. You are fighting and killing yourselves over land which those who are not God's special people have in abundance. And what land are you fighting over? A desert! It is all very laughable.'

'The landless are God's people while the landlords are the gentiles and philistines. The bastard inherits while the son is disinherited. The prince is trekking while the beggar is riding a horse. All these sound strange,' said another conferee.

Passage Seventeen

God is the landlord of the earth while man and other creatures are his tenants was the topic of the fifth day of the conference. 'God created the earth and all things in it,' said an angel. 'As the creator of the earth, he built the earth. The world is a house. God is the landlord. Human beings, beasts and birds are mere tenants.'

'There is no light in the house,' someone hissed.

'You forget the sun,' another person quipped.

'There is no water,' someone jeered.

'You forget the seas, the oceans and the rivers?' another person retorted.

'I mean pipe-borne, drinkable water.'

'Fishes are drinking sea, ocean and river water. I have never heard them complaining of typhoid,' someone rejoined.

'It is such a fearsome thing being the tenant of a fearsome character like God,' said a conferee.

'Well, I don't feel the way you feel,' said another conferee. 'I feel great being the tenant of a great guy like God. That's how I feel right now.

Oh, no; that's not the only way I feel. I feel awful that God puts up with loathsome characters like us as tenants.'

The conference once more devolved into a free for all talk.

'We are not only tenants of God in the world; we are his tenants in the body. We are double tenants and he is a double landlord.'

'As landlord, God has onerous responsibilities. He has to keep the house in a hospitable, livable and tenantable state of repairs. Can you honestly say he has been doing so?'

'I can't answer that question until I know what you mean by hospitable, livable and tenantable state of repairs.'

'A hospitable, livable and tenantable state of repairs is making sure there is sufficient rain on earth, no violent winds, no destructive thunder, no mosquitoes, no hyenas, no vultures, no rats and no flies.'

'You are forgetting man is something of a rat. Being a rat, he naturally attracts rats. God can't be accountable for that.'

'Ordinarily he wouldn't have been accountable for that if he had not created man as a rat.'

'God may do his best to keep his house in a hospitable and livable state. But man can undermine his efforts. Man is a pig. This has been God's headache.'

'As a tenant, man has the responsibility of paying his rents. I don't think he has been faithful in doing so.'

'How do we pay our rents?'

'You see what I am saying.'

'The same way you pay tithes.'

'By worshipping the landlord – the lord of host, hosting you.'

'That's too servile a rent to extract.'

'More of a cheap rent to pay, if you ask me.'

'No one is asking you; so, shut up.'

'Man has the responsibility of not challenging the title of his landlord.'

'This is one covenant man has not always kept. He has always challenged the title of his landlord by claiming to be landlord.'

'Ordinarily, a breach of this covenant attracts forfeiture. But God has always been magnanimous enough not to hold man to strict observance of this covenant.'

'Man also has the duty of keeping the house clean.'

'Well, he has been doing the best a pig can to keep its piggery in a clean state.'

'Most of us deserve quit notices.'

'No, most of us should be ejected without the courtesy of quit notice.'

'God is practicing absentee landlordism.'

'Does that entitle you not to be paying your rent?'

Passage Eighteen

In heaven some angels saw the conference as a talk-shop rather than a workshop. A day to the end of the conference, three angels met and began talking about the conference.

'Do you think the ongoing conference is such a smart idea?' asked the first angel.

'Honestly, I don't think it is. What is it that the conference is discussing that we couldn't have and found a solution to?' said the second angel.

'Talking about discussion and finding solutions, in the end, who found the solution to the problem God called the conference?' asked the first angel.

'An angel,' replied the second angel.

'You see what I mean.'

'How can it ever happen that guys from a barren earth will have more brains than us in a fertile heaven?'

'I wonder.'

'Look at the humiliation of having to serve characters like these.'

'Look at the cost.'

'I wonder why God sometimes takes decisions without conferring with anyone.'

'Do you suspect the devil influenced him to call the conference? You know that guy will stop at nothing to ridicule God.'

'There may be something in what you are saying. If the devil is not behind the conference, why did many inmates of hell sneak into it?'

'No, I don't think the devil has a hand in this. He is bad no doubt. But it does not mean he is behind everything we think is bad,' said the third angel who so far had not spoken.

'You can imagine the rascals going back to earth thinking heaven needs them to solve its problems,' said the first angel.

'But why should they think so when they were not the ones who proffered the solution?' said the third angel.

'I wonder,' said the second angel.

'God will eventually find that this conference cost him more than just feeding and accommodation. It cost him his Godliness. Humans will begin to wonder if he is that powerful. Familiarity breeds contempt you know,' said the first angel.

'I think the conference has served a useful purpose,' said the third angel. 'Because of the conference, the earth has been able to table before God its grouse and grievances against itself, and its thoughts about God. But for the conference, none of these would have happened.'

'And what is the usefulness of these things you are babbling about happening?' asked the first angel. 'Yes, they have happened. What is the remarkable gain to heaven in their happening?'

'You always talk of gain as if you are a merchant,' said the third angel. 'Well, if you are a merchant, I don't think the conference has been all loss for God and heaven. By inviting the earth to heaven to deliberate on matters of common interest, God has shown he is a democrat.'

'And what is the use of showing you are a democrat to an incurable cynic and nihilist?' the first angel interjected. 'Man is a cynic and a nihilist. Showing him you are a democrat is like casting pearls before swine.'

'Well, I don't think so,' said the third angel. 'Neither do I think the earth will think less of God because he invited it to heaven. While here no man has seen his face, and when they wanted to mess up, he reminded them of who he is. No, it is not all loss for heaven. I think we gained something.'

'I agree with you there,' said the second angel. 'In fact, those who before now doubted there is God now know there is God. In the conference, they saw and felt his presence.'

'The only question is whether their knowledge will make a difference in their behavior,' said the first angel. 'Men are pigs and will remain so whatever washing you give them because they are pigs at heart. They are ...'

'Ssh...' interposed the third angel. 'We should not forget we are angels: pious beings from who foul language would not be heard; meek beings in whose mouths butter would not melt. What if someone is eavesdropping on us? What will he think of us? The way we are talking, don't you think he will be wondering if he is in hell listening to demons and not in heaven listening to angels? What we are saying sounds demonic than angelic.'

'Just now I don't care where anyone listening in will think he is or who he is listening to,' said the first angel.

'Well, I care, and I believe God also cares,' said the third angel.

'I also care in a way,' said the second angel.

'Anyone, particularly from the earth, lurking about eavesdropping on us is a rat and I don't give a hoot about rats,' said the first angel with fervor.

'Well, perhaps I also don't care about rats, but God does,' said the third angel. 'We should always be wary of offending his feelings.'

'I agree with you there,' said the second angel. 'We are courtiers in God's court and should do only what pleases him.'

Passage Nineteen

The conference ended on the fifth day. Like every conference, there were rapporteurs who prepared a communiqué. Conferees and plenipotentiaries from the earth were expected to implement the resolutions of the conference when they get back to earth. The conference also produced a charter containing these resolutions:

i. Aliens from Fagasso would be invited to engage invading aliens from Thongos.
ii. Whites should give blacks a better deal and blacks should improve their attitude.
iii. Arabs and Israelis should listen to the devil less.
iv. Fanatics should not fight for God; God will fight for himself.
v. Terrorists are on their own.
vi. Killing terrorists is sanctioned by God.

After the conference, God held a press conference with journalists from the earth. Many questions were fielded and answers provided:

'This is the first world conference in heaven; will there be similar conferences in future?'

'It depends on needs.'

'What were the needs for this conference?'

'They are contained in the communiqué.'

'Did conferees from the world behave well during the conference?'

'They behaved the best way they were capable of and heaven did the best it could to put up with nuisances.'

www.ingramcontent.com/pod-product-compliance
Lightning Source LLC
Chambersburg PA
CBHW022010170726

47994CB00023B/2906